HAMLE'
IN
BALTIMORE

BY

PAVEL CERNY

ILLUSTRATIONS

BY

MANUEL WITTMAN

FROM A HEART LAID BARE SERIES

To order additional copies of this book, contact:
Xlibris
844-714-8691
www.Xlibris.com
Orders@Xlibris.com

ISBN: 978-1-6641-5864-1 (sc)
ISBN: 978-1-6641-5865-8 (hc)
ISBN: 978-1-6641-5863-4 (e)

Print information available on the last page

Rev. date: 02/23/2021

This horror and vampire story attempts to recreate the influences on the later work of Edgar Alan Poe as seen from the point of view of a five-year-old Edgar. It is wholly a book of fiction. Poe was born in 1809. His father left the family a year later and his mother died when he was two.

1) The excerpts of the plays are from "Romeo and Juliet" and from "The Tragedie of Hamlet, Prince of Denmarke", both by Wiliam Shakespeare.

HAMLET IN BALTIMORE

THE YEAR IS 1814. Moody autumn weather, with the last yellow and red leaves being torn off their branches by wind, is present. The wind blew away all the clouds and so now the pale full moon reigns supreme.

Most of the center of the city of Baltimore consists of two and three story red brick buildings. Smoke is rising out of the many chimneys as the cold chills the bones inside the rooms at night. Several taller buildings stand on the main square, among them the Swan Theatre. Inside, on the stage of this ornate playhouse in the old part of Baltimore, actors perform Shakespeare's *Romeo and Juliet*. The theater's director, Mr. Olivier Reynolds—a well preserved fifty-five-year-old man with salt and pepper hair, sensuous lips, and a thin mustache above them—is playing the Prince of Verona

PRINCE

"A glooming peace this morning with

it brings, The sun for sorrow will not

show his head; Go hence to

have more talk of these sad things;

Some shall be pardon'd and some

punished, For never was a story of

more woe, Then this of Juliet and

her Romeo."

Some of the actors are dressed in Elizabethan garb, others are wearing better contemporary clothes, as was the fashion of the time. While the curtain falls, theatre supernumeraries slowly lower Mrs. Elisabeth Poe, playing Juliet, and Mr. Jason Lowell, playing Romeo, from their pretend "catafalques," and carry them in a funeral procession. This is met with enthusiastic applause from the audience. The front rows of the theater are occupied by the well-to-do patrons, while the poorer ones—especially the students—stand in the back of the balcony, so high as to give the area the name, "Gods."

Mrs. Poe, an ethereal beauty with translucent complexion framed by long black hair, and with large black eyes, smiles at Mr. Lowell, the tall blond male star of the theater company. "We made it." she declares.

"Yes," he replies. "This was our eighth performance."

Mr. Lowell, an easy going man from the south, is followed by the jealous eyes of Mrs. Poe's husband, the skinny Mr. David Poe, who was one of the actors lowering her to the floor. Mrs. Poe and the handsome Mr. Lowell are almost a decade his junior. Mrs. Poe notices her husband's glowering look, and decides to change the conversation. "You have to watch out, David! You have torn my dress."

"Well, you shouldn't bloody move when we are taking you down."

Meanwhile, continuous applause is heard from the audience. The stage manager, a short man with a hump and strong hands, pulls down on the lever that makes the curtain rise again. All the actors, smiling, take a bow. Someone in the audience throws a bouquet of pink camellias to Mrs. Poe, who graciously picks it up and holds it to her ivory bosom.

As the actors walk from the stage to their casting rooms, they stop by the bulletin board where the casting for the upcoming production of *The Tragedy of Hamlet, The King of Denmark* is posted. Mrs. Poe is full of anticipation, but she is stopped on her way by Reynolds.

"That was excellent, my dear Mrs. Poe. I believe that was the best Juliet you ever played. I myself could hardly constrain tears from coming to my eyes. One of these days I'll take you away from here and make you a diva in Paris and London." They both laugh at the little joke and Mr. Reynolds releases Mrs. Poe to satisfy her curiosity about the role in which she was cast. She gets to the bulletin board, just as her husband is finished scanning it. He found under the name Mr. David Poe the roles of "Osric-a Courtier" and "Understudy for the Male Roles." He walks out of the crowd of actors surrounding the list, full of anger.. Mrs. Poe takes a short look at the list just glimpsing her name next to "Ophelia," and runs after her husband who is yelling loud enough for everyone to hear him.

"Again, the damned Reynolds has done it to me again."

"David, dear, don't make a spectacle of yourself." pleaded Mrs. Poe.

"That's about the only spectacle I shall make in this company. Ophelia, it's easy for you to talk, but I? In the next play, I'll end up playing the Third Spear Carrier with scarcely any lines at all. And who will be playing the lead again? Lowell! Why can't I play a lead for once? I would give my life to be able to play Hamlet! I have the looks, I am still the right age. I even know the role by heart…"

"Just be patient," interrupted Mrs. Poe calmly. "You will still play them all."

"Patient? I was already told I was too old for Romeo. Soon I will miss Hamlet and the Scottish play. What should I wait for? Lear?"

He is close to tears. After a short while, giving Mr. Poe a chance to calm down, Mrs. Poe quietly asks, "Do you want me to talk to Mr. Reynolds?"

This just makes Mr. Poe even more annoyed. "I don't need a woman to talk for me. Why should you care anyway? They say you make a perfect couple on stage—Lowell and you. You have read the *Gazette*."

"Please David. You know I would love to play opposite you."

"Let's not waste more words. I'll see you in the morning. I think I'll stop by the pub for a while." Mr. Poe retorts shortly.

"Please stay with me. There is no performance tomorrow, only rehearsal in the morning. Let us all go somewhere for an outing."

"I don't feel like it. Good night." Poe hands his wife the hat and jacket he was wearing for tonight's play, puts on his own coat, and runs out through the actor's entrance door to the theater. Mrs. Poe goes to her dressing room, where little Edgar, their five-year-old son, is waiting with their black nanny, Letitia. Edgar, a handsome young boy with dark hair and greenish eyes, is holding a small black cat in his lap.

"Edgar, where did you find it?" asks Letitia. Letitia is a little corpulent for her comparatively young age, but she is full of energy and is eager to help.

"Edgar, where did you find that cat?" adds Mrs. Poe.

"It has come Madam, just a while ago, and Mr. Eddy has played with it ever since."

Mrs. Poe has hardly heard the answer as she is preoccupied with changing from Juliet's costume, a shabby everyday frock. "We'll go now, Letitia. That was the last of

Romeo and Juliet. It's late and Edgar should have already been sleeping. Eddy, say good night to the cat. It will stay here in the theatre."

Eddy reluctantly put the animal on the ground and the cat immediately skedaddles away.

"Goodbye, kitty." he calls after the retreating animal.

It is already late at night when Mrs. Poe and Letitia walk briskly to the house across the street from the theatre where the Poe's are renting a flat. The streets are deserted except for an occasional carriage. Letitia carries a lantern, even though the night is lit by the full moon. Mrs. Poe carries Eddy in her arms, who is the only one to notice that the cat is following them. She unlocks the door while Letitia holds the light for her to see. Something makes a noise by Mrs. Poe's legs.

"Ah! Oh, it was just the cat. Look Eddy, it followed us home. Poor kitty, you must be hungry, right? Letitia, I'll put Eddy to bed and you find some milk for the cat in the meantime."

Eddy is already fast asleep when Mrs. Poe pulls up the quilt that covers him. The cat fawns by Mrs. Poe's legs, satisfied.

It is late at night, but Mr. Poe is still not at home. The bedroom is drowning in moonlight. A couple of ravens sit on a branch of a chestnut tree in front of the window, their silhouette contrasting with the full moon. Mrs. Poe is breathing heavily. Her coverlet fell off the bed earlier, and now she lies with only a thin sheet covering her lithe body. Suddenly, a tall shadow of a tall man looks over the walls. It grows ever larger as it approaches the sleeping woman. She turns in her sleep, as if bothered by a nightmare. The silhouette of a man in a black coat is approaching her stealthily when Mrs. Poe sits up. The house is submerged in silence. The shadowy man is gone.

"Letitia, can't you hear Master Eddy crying? What time is it? Mr. Poe is still not home yet." she calls out. Without waiting for an answer, she staggers out into the next room to pick up the crying child. The bedroom appears otherwise empty, except for the black cat sitting on the windowsill.

The next day, it is the time for fitting costumes for the new production. Most of them are just old costumes being re-sewn and altered. While Letitia is helping the dressmaker with a pin cushion on her wrist to pin Mrs. Poe's white brocade dress for Ophelia, Mr. Poe is sleeping off last night's escapades on the sofa in the adjoining part of the dressing room. Eddy is supposed to be in his father's care, but he is used to seeing his father prostrate and disheveled. He feels lonely since no one pays attention to him.

"Papa, do you want to pet my new cat?" Eddy asks.

Mr. Poe opens his bleary eyes, but then he turns towards the wall. Eddy is chasing the large black cat under the table and behind the folding screen. The cat tries to run away, but Eddy won't let her. Suddenly, the cat starts running towards the partially open door. Eddy, screaming with joy, grabs the lamp off the table and follows her.

Eddy has never been under the stage. Lit by the light of his lantern, the boy can see a huge wooden cog used to turn the turntable for the stage. In the corner, there are several large crates and one that looks like a coffin. Suddenly, something flashes by and all that Eddy can see is that the object has disappeared behind the coffin. Then a sound of a frightened cat can be heard echoing through the underground. Eddy goes to investigate whether the cat has disappeared in the coffin. He sees something blinking inside, looking like the green eyes of the cat, and he manages to move a box to the coffin so that he can climb in and investigate. Just as he is raising his other leg to get inside, his lantern falls on the floor, breaks to smithereens, and the room is plunged into darkness. Eddy can hear strange squeaking noises as if the revolving stage has started moving. He is standing inside the open coffin, with everything around him buried by darkness. Then, the squeaking becomes high pitched. He starts crying.

Mrs. Poe is done with her fittings. She grabs the embroidered shawl she loves so much and puts it around her shoulders. She finds Mr. Poe lying on the bed in a stupor, staring at the ceiling. The room is getting dark because the kerosene in the lamp on the table is low. One of Mr. Poe's feet hangs shoeless over the edge of the daybed.

"David, where did Eddy go?" Mrs. Poe inquires.

Mr. Poe is not sure what his wife is talking about, but he concentrates just enough to discern the note of alarm in her voice.

"He was just here, dear. Over there, playing with the cat. Eddy? Eddy?"

Soon both of Eddy's parents are joined by other actors, including Mr. Lowell, who still wears the doublet from his black velvet Hamlet rehearsal costume. They search all the dressing rooms and the stage. People call out in louder and louder voices, "Eddy!! EDDY!" Then Anthony, a young novice actor, has an idea.

"Are you sure he didn't run out to the street, following that beast?"

Most of the actors run to the actor's exit. It is already dark outside, but some of the actors brought along lanterns and torches. They spread around to look around the neighboring houses, but there is no sign of the child. Mr. Lowell notices that Mrs. Poe is not with his group, and he runs to her dressing room, where he finds her with her head laid down on the dressing room table, crying. "Don't worry Mrs. Poe. Eddy will be just fine. Boys are sometimes curious." He turns to Leticia, who is standing hopelessly in the corner, and asks, ""How come you were not with your young master?"

Mrs. Poe dries her eyes. "She was helping me with pinning the hem of my dress, it was David who was to take care of Eddy."

With her cried-out eyes, she looks even more beautiful than usual, but Mr. Lowell doesn't have time to admire her now. "Don't worry," Mr. Lowell reassures. "He will be just fine. Boys sometimes become curious. Now, Letitia, take care of your mistress!"

He runs out of the dressing room and starts climbing the rope ladder that leads to the catwalk—the wooden bridge above the stage. The stage is darkened, lit only by a large kerosene lantern which is serving as the ghost light standing in the stage center. Currently, it is clear that there is no one on it. Mr. Lowell comes down again and starts climbing the creaking wooden steps leading to the space where the flats are being stored. He finds a small metal door at the bottom of the floor. He tries to open it, but his efforts are in vain. It seems to him that he can hear the muffled cries of a child. He finds a crowbar and tries to break the lock. Just at that moment, the door suddenly opens and out comes Mr. Reynolds, carrying Edgar. Reynolds has a smirk on his face.

"I've found him under the stage," he announces.

Mr. Lowell attempts to take Edgar in his arms, but Reynolds just passes by him, carrying the child. He takes long strides to get to Mrs. Poe's dressing room. Mr. Lowell hardly has time to step aside so that Reynolds, while carrying the child, does not crash into him.

Mrs. Poe is so overjoyed by seeing her son that she doesn't even ask any question of Eddy's savior. "Eddy, darling, where have you been? And look at your clothes, they are all full of dirt." In response, Eddy just starts crying again.

"Thank you Mr. Reynolds. Thank you for bringing Eddy back. I am forever beholden to you. I don't know how to show you my gratitude."

Mr. Reynolds carefully hands Eddy to Letitia and takes Mrs. Poe by her chin.

"Later, Mrs. Poe, later." he tells her. He then disappears so fast that the two women, both preoccupied by the crying child, hardly notice.

The rehearsal is running longer today, and the lamp on the table, covered by a black shawl with embroidered red poppies, is flickering. Mrs. Poe is gently holding Eddy, who has by now been scrubbed clean and is wearing his nightgown.

"And then the kitty jumped into that big black box and disappeared!" he explains forcefully. "And then someone took the lamp out of my hand."

There is a knocking on the door and Mr. Lowell enters. He stands quietly by the door, not wanting to disturb.

"Eddy, who would do a thing like that?" says Mrs. Poe, smiling.

Letitia makes a sign of a cross over her breast. "Stranger things have happened, madam."

"Oh Letitia, now you start with your superstitions too."

"I couldn't see, but I felt someone pulling on that lamp. I did. I tell you."

A smile appears on Mrs. Poe's lips. It is the first sign of relaxation since Eddy's disappearance. She looks up and notices Mr. Lowell, standing nearby, then starts laughing and cuddling the child. "Children, nowadays. They have such imaginations!"

Mr. Lowell's face remained serious. "Don't laugh at him. This is a spooky place. I wouldn't be surprised to find out it was haunted." Letitia's eyes widen, but Mr. Lowell turns to the boy. "Tell me, Eddy. How long before I came did Mr. Reynolds find you?"

"I heard someone pounding on the door, and then Mr. Reynolds lifted me and said, "Here you are. This will please your mother.""

"You mean he was in the room with you?" asked Mr. Lowell.

"I sure didn't see him coming in. Only that cat jumping on the box."

Mrs. Poe looks at Mr. Lowell perplexed. "I told you—children's imagination." Her embarrassment makes her charming, and Mr. Lowell feels ill at ease, but Letitia laughs at Mrs. Poe's little joke. Then, at that moment, the door flies open and Mr. Poe runs in.

"So it's true, He's here and nobody told me." He turns to the boy. "Where were you? Don't ever leave without permission." He starts beating Eddy. Mr. Lowell tries to intervene.

"Leave him, Mr. Poe. It wasn't the boy's fault."

"I would appreciate it if you did not get mixed up in my domestic affairs. Kindly leave now. Here I play the lead!"

Mr. Lowell wants to answer, but then he just makes a turn and walks out of the room.

Letitia wants to pick up the crying boy, but Mr. Poe turns around and starts beating her as well. "Here, you lazy hag. It was all your fault in the first place. Is that how you take care of your master? I should send you back from where you came." Letitia tries to cover her head with her arms, but Mr. Poe is relentless until Mrs. Poe stops him. "David, please. You are indisposed. Please go home and wait for us."

Mr. Poe looks around and then he walks out, slamming the door behind him. Little Edgar is hiding in the corner of the room. His face is sticky with tears and dirt.

Winter is coming and the nights are becoming longer. Red maple trees in the square in front of the theatre are bare. Long gone is their brilliant red magnificence. Only the occasional pine still stands with its needles revolting against the winds. Once the audiences for the long running *Romeo and Juliet* started thinning, the actors went into rehearsals for the long advertised production of *Hamlet*. Mr. Lowell plays the Prince of Denmark, and his good blond looks are perfect for the part. Mrs. Poe's pale complexion and long dark hair compliment the lace dress she is wearing. The two of them really look good together.

The stage manager is lighting some footlights at the edge of the stage. Actors stand patiently in the wings, waiting for their cues. The prompter is reading the text, penciling in the cuts that Mr. Reynolds, the play's director, made. Mr. Poe, in partial armor, is watching a group of stage hands playing the newfangled game of poker. Occasionally, he glances at the stage where the entry of the players is being rehearsed. Mr. Lowell and Mrs. Poe, as Hamlet and Ophelia, are watching the troupe of actors invited to the Elsinor

Castle by Hamlet. Mr. Jackman plays the director of the group of itinerant actors who arrived at the palace at the invitation of Hamlet.

Most of the stage is empty. Only Mrs. Poe's Ophelia sits on a rug covered raiser. Mr. Lowell walks up to her.

HAMLET

Lady, shall I lie in your lap?

OPHELIA

No my Lord.

HAMLET

I mean my head upon your lap.

OPHELIA

Ay my Lord.

The men sitting by the card table next to where Mr. Poe is standing stop their game for a second. One of the card players, a tall man with ruddy cheeks, puts his cards on the table (with their backside to the top) and turns around in his chair to see better. "Wait men," he proclaims. "I want to see this one. 'Head upon your lap...' Get it?" Both he and another card player stand up, and giggling, approach the stage to see the proceeding better. Lowell buries his head in Mrs. Poe's lap, slowly and passionately. Suddenly, yelling loudly, while tripping over his spear, Mr. Poe walks on the stage.

"That is not how the play should be done. He should just lean against her knee. This kind of behavior is unacceptable in a decent theatre." The prompter starts searching the book to find the lines of the corresponding speech.

Inside the darkened auditorium, Mr. Reynolds is watching the rehearsal from the fifth row of the otherwise empty theatre. He is watching the commotion on the stage with a slight smile. Then he yells so that his voice carries all the way to the stage. "You are right, Mr. Poe."

He stops and watches the impact his sentence had on his actors. Then, he continues loud enough as to reach all the actors and stage hands. "Mr. Lowell shall restrain himself from making any movements suggestive of lack of morals. It detracts from the text and would offend the gentler souls in our audience."

Mr. Lowell is in shock at first, but then he decides to fight the order. He starts yelling down to the empty audience seats. "But it says so just in the very next verse. 'That's fair thought to lie between maid's legs.'"

Mr. Poe, who has already read his few lines for the small part of Osric, does not worry about the other claptrap happening while he is off stage. He is drinking some mulled hot hard cider while awaiting now for his next cue, and suddenly gets involved in the proceedings. "I shall not permit it to be said about my wife." His face turns red with anger.

By then, Mrs. Poe is feeling embarrassed that the whole company is witness to the two men's fight over her. "David, it says so in the play."

Mr. Reynolds sees an opening for an opportunity to get rid of the pesky Mr. Poe who stands in the way of his objectives. "No, no, Mrs. Poe. Your husband has a point there. Let us cut the offending line in the name of all the fair ladies that shall visit our play."

Mr. Lowell usually has an even temperament, but such nonsense makes him angry too.

"But that is ridiculous, this is the greatest of all plays! You are cutting lines written by William Shakespeare! Either we do it as it is written or I don't do it."

Surprisingly, Mr. Reynolds stays unmoved. "May I talk to you privately, Mr. Lowell?"

Lowell jumps off the stage in the aisle and comes to where Reynolds sits. Reynolds has a contemptuous smile on his narrow lips.

"Mr. Lowell, let us make one thing clear. You and I are not here to discuss the literary merits of the play. We are here to sell tickets. They pay my bills and yours, Mr. Lowell."

"But how can you listen to an idiot like Poe?

"Mr. Poe may not have your intellectual brilliance, but in that, he is similar to our audiences. If you therefore know of a better way to make a living, I suggest that you should try it. If you choose to stay with us, you go back on that stage now."

Lowell looks around. Though they couldn't hear the whispered sentences, many actors watched the exchange from the stage. He has been had. He fell in Reynolds' trap. "I didn't mean to anger you, Mr. Reynolds."

"I am too tired. I didn't get much sleep. I can't afford having Poe leave and take his wife with him."

Lowell looks at his director and really, Reynold's face is very pale and haggard. He climbs up the stage again. Mr. Reynolds was not done creating discipline among his ensemble.

"And Mr. Poe shall kindly restrain from any further interruptions. It is my duty to decide what is permissible in my theatre."

"But it had to do with my wife!" exclaimed Mr. Poe. His protests were in vain. Reynolds put on the theatre director's hat and would no longer listen to any silly quarrels.

"I understand this, but this is not the time, with a week until the opening. Shall we?" His voice sounds tired and the other actors slowly return to their positions on stage. The ones who had no business in the scene walk back to the wings of the stage. Lowell, as Hamlet, now keeping a careful distance, sits next to his Ophelia. His voice as Hamlet is suddenly hesitant.

HAMLET

Lady, shall I lie in your lap?

Mrs. Poe is not answering. There are tears in her eyes. The prompter thinking that she has forgotten her lines and whispers, "No, my Lord."

Meanwhile, Eddy is being put in bed by the faithful Letitia. It is raining behind the window. It seems as if the sky was crying.

"Why was daddy upset, Letitia?"

"Nothing, angel. Nothing important. Do not worry. Letitia will tell you a story."

"Yes, yes. But make it scary again. I like to be scared."

"Alright, but you try to close your eyes. Your parents won't be home for a while and you better be asleep when they come."

"What is your story for tonight? Magicians and witches?

"Let me try to remember the story. Don't forget, keep your eyes closed. Well, let me see. It is the story of Carmella Lee. She was a beautiful girl. Skin black like ebony. Teeth like pearls…"

"Like you, Letitia?

"Yes. Just like me. Teeth like pearls and eyes shining like icicles. Well, this Carmella Lee once met a handsome officer from the cavalry. He had a mustache like horns of an ox, and arms like a bear. He just winked his eyes at her, and she fell head over heels for him. Little did she know that he would be her ruination. He brought Carmella Lee flowers, and to her mommy too.

He gave Carmella a ring one night, but when she came home in the morning, she was a different girl. She had a mark on her neck. She also had a mark in her heart. Ever since that night, Carmella Lee was disappearing at night and they…"

Eddy turns around towards the wall. He closes his eyes and immediately sleeps. Letitia covers the child with a quilt she made for him. She sits down next to Eddy. Suddenly, the sky lights up with lightning. A few seconds later, a majestic thunder is heard. Letitia genuflects and makes a sigh of the cross.

Mrs. Poe is just returning to her dressing room from the stage when she hears the thunder. She runs to her dressing room. To her surprise, her chair by the make-up mirror is occupied by Mr. Reynolds, who is waiting for her. He asks her, "Are you surprised to see me here, my dear? I came looking for your husband."

"He went to the Lion's Head." answers Mrs. Poe.

"Drinking again? Tsk, tsk. How about you? Are you satisfied with the role I chose for you?"

"Yes! I have dreamt about playing Ophelia for a long time. I just wish I could find my husband just as satisfied with the part he got as I am with mine."

"Forget about your husband—he is a drunken sot. I keep him in the company only because of you."

"If he goes anywhere, I will have to follow. I meant it when I said that we could leave tomorrow." Mrs. Poe stops in her tracks. She considered their small talk just that, a small talk. Until now, Mr. Reynolds' overtures were just said in jest after all. Or weren't they? She looks at Reynold as if she could read his real intentions from his eyes. His eyes are just narrowed, like those of a cat—but not a cat that would be satisfied with a little scratching behind the ears.

"Remember what I said? First, we would move our production to the Chestnut Street Theatre. Then, London, Paris, and Rome." He stands in front of her and wants to kiss her, but at that very moment, someone knocks on the door. They hear the voice of Mr. Lowell behind the door, which is very urgent.

"Mrs. Poe. Please open."

Reynold puts a finger on his thin lips and motions her not to mention his presence. Mrs. Poe is flustered. She gathers her wits and with the most natural voice she is able to gather, she yells to the person outside, "Who is it?"

"It is me. Mr. Lowell."

"Oh, just one second. I shall open presently."

"I need to talk to you urgently." Mr. Lowell responds through the door.

Mrs. Poe is panicking by now. She whispers to her visitor, "Mr. Reynolds, you will have to go now. People would start talking, with the two of us in a locked room."

Reynolds is clearly annoyed. "Blasted Lowell, forever in my way." He doesn't seem to worry about his star's good name. After a short while, Mr. Lowell knocks on the door again. "I have something to tell you about Reynolds." he entreats again.

Mrs. Poe is getting desperate. Reynolds looks around the room to look for a solution to the locked room problem. He whispers so that Mr. Lowell can't hear him. "Yes, you are right. It is time to withdraw. If this were a play, the directions would say, 'Exit Mr. Reynolds.'" Laughing, he walks to a tall mirror. After touching the frame, the mirror opens and reveals a secret passageway. Just as he enters the corridor, Lowell manages to break down the door.

"He was here! He stood in front of this mirror, but there was no reflection of him!"

Mrs. Poe exclaims as she gathers her acting talent.

Lowell exclaims, "What are you talking about? Forgive me my entrance. I could hear his voice. That's why I was so bold."

Mrs. Poe is feeling unwell. An unknown secret passage leading straight to her dressing room? Reynolds with his strange proposal? Who does he think she is? Her thoughts are disjointed, mirroring how she is feeling inside. And Mr. Lowell is unrelenting:

"Believe me, Reynolds is dangerous. He is not one of us. Remember when you laughed at Eddy's story about the box in which his cat has disappeared? Well, today while you were rehearsing your mad scene, I ventured under the stage. There it was—a coffin."

"Mr. Lowell, that could have been a prop from some long-forgotten play." Mrs. Poe calmly explained.

"You may be right, but have you ever seen Reynolds during the daytime? What do we know about his life outside these walls?"

"I reckon this is the wildest story I have ever heard. Or did I perhaps detect a trace of jealousy in your voice?" She returns to her make up table and starts brushing her long hair.

"Don't laugh at me, Elisabeth. Forgive me for being so bold as to use your Christian name. I know that you've suspected for a long time now. You know that I never said a word and will never come between you and your husband. Now I must. If not for yourself, then in the name of little Edgar. Will you do me a favor?" He removes a silver cross on a chain from his neck. "Please wear it always. It will keep you safe."

"How sweet of you. It is lovely. I'll wear it always." While Lowell puts the chain around her neck, a black cat is watching from behind the folding screen in the corner.

It is a busy night at the Lion's Head Pub in Baltimore. Merchants are discussing their trade, bricklayers are laughing with their wenches, and there is even a captain of a ship crisscrossing the Chesapeake Bay enjoying himself. Mr. Poe is already quite drunk, but Reynolds standing next to him keeps filling his glass from a bottle of rye sitting on the table in front of them. "You are a clever fellow, David. You have talent. Is there any reason why you shouldn't play larger roles? You have seen how impertinent Mr. Lowell has been. I have a good mind to replace him. Just to show him. If he had a smaller part, I would have fired him on the spot."

"But he is playing Hamlet."

"Yes, that's the problem—the time it would take to find someone who knows the lines, someone who watched the rehearsals and knows where he should stand. Well, there goes that idea."

Mr. Poe can hardly wait for Reynolds to finish his line. He almost cries out, "I know it all. I watched all the rehearsals."

Mr. Reynolds' lips turn into a disdainful smile. "And I thought you'd disappoint me. Then welcome aboard, sweet prince. He laughs again. Now, have another drink. It is on me—I pay."

Mr. Poe suddenly becomes dead serious. "No, Mr. Reynolds, not if I am to play Hamlet. I shall drink no more."

He lifts his glass and pours the contents onto the floor.

Tonight, the scene of "Gonzaga's Murder" from Hamlet is being rehearsed. There is a small wooden stage on top of the theatre's stage. The rehearsal is going on without a hitch. The actors who are performing the roles of the players are reciting the play requested by the Prince of Denmark. The older actor entrusted with the role of the Player King is the same one who played Hamlet's father the King. Here, he is playing the dramatized role that should irritate the new king, Hamlet's uncle and at the same time step-father. It is the scene of the poisoned King saying his goodbyes before dying.

PLAYER KING

"Faith, I must leave thee, love,

and my operant powers their

functions leave to do; And thou

shalt live in this fair world

happily one as kind. For husband

shalt though"

Mrs. Poe slides into the auditorium seat next to Reynolds. "You wanted to see me, Mr. Reynolds?"

Mr. Reynolds, smiles at her with his thin lips and eyes that become as narrow as those of a cat before attack. We do not hear his answer, as the male acting as the queen according to the conventions of the Elizabethan theater, starts with her speech.

PLAYER QUEEN

"O, confound the rest! Such love

must needs be treason in my

breast; In second husband let

me to be accurst! None we the second

but who kill'd the first."

There is a pause. No one says the following line, even though the prompter keeps whispering feverishly, "Wormwood, wormwood!" There is still nothing. The actors stop and keep looking around for Lowell to say Hamlet's lines. Finally the young actor, who was portraying Player Ophelia, steps across the ramp to talk to Reynolds. Reynolds doesn't seem to notice him as his attention is given to Mrs. Poe in the seat next to him. Finally, the young actor with a fairly high pitched voice interrupts Reynolds.

"Mr. Lowell is missing."

Reynolds smiles and stands up, facing the stage. "We have some casting changes. Mr. Poe is taking over the role of Hamlet. Mr. Lowell refused the smaller roles that I felt were better suited to his abilities and decided to part with our company. We wish him much luck elsewhere. Alright, shall we start with the Player Queen's speech again? The actors on and off stage are whispering among themselves. Reynolds triumphantly sits down again next to Mrs. Poe.

"Satisfied?

Mrs. Poe is not sure how to answer. She is trying to make sense of what's happening. How will this improve her relationship with her husband, who was thirsting after a big role ever since the two of them became members of the troupe over two years ago? What will this news mean for her position as the star of Mr. Reynolds' company? Will she be in any way obliged now to Reynolds? "Thank you. David will be so happy. Though I feel sorry for poor Mr. Lowell."

"What's Lowell to you? Just another poor actor. For that matter, what's David Poe to you? When will you finally understand that your future lies with me? Did you consider my proposition?"

Mrs. Poe is bewildered. Yes, the offer of an international career is inviting, but at what price? "I couldn't leave my husband. I told you I was a married woman." She protests weakly, only afterwards realizing that she forgot the argument that she is also a mother to a small boy. At that same moment, just for a few seconds, the director's attention is attracted to the action on stage.

PLAYER QUEEN

"The instance that second marriage

would move, Are base respects of

thrift, but none of love; A second

time I kill my husband dead, When

second husband kisses me in bed.

PLAYER KING

I do believe you think what now

you speak.”

Mr. Reynolds returns to the original subject of their conversation. “I told you. I cannot wait. My time is running short.”

“I don't understand you.” Mrs. Poe replies, bewildered.

“You know I am sickly. Look at me. I need to take a cure. Let's leave together.”

“I couldn't do that. I would be sorely missed.”

By now Reynolds is getting angry and exasperated. “You use your marriage as a shield. Is it the ‘till death do us part?’ What if your husband was gone? Would you come with me then?”

“What are you suggesting?” asks Mrs. Poe. “You couldn't really mean that.”

Reynolds feigns a hearty laughter. “I told you I was joking.” Suddenly, he stops mid-sentence to ask, “What's that on your neck? A new chain? From Mr. Poe?”

Mrs. Poe is searching for a response. “No, it was a gift.” She blushes as she replies.

“Careful. I don't allow competition.” Mr. Reynolds responds coldly. He laughs again, but it is a fake, cold laughter.

Mrs. Poe is confused by their conversation, but Reynolds is again engaged by watching his actors.

PLAYER KING

“Our thoughts are ours, their ends

none of ours. So think thou wilt

no second husband we: But die

thy thoughts when thy first lord

is dead.”

Mrs. Poe feels like a prisoner of Reynold's remarks. She gets up from the seat next to Reynolds and runs out of the theatre.

The anticipated night has arrived. Signs in front of The Swan Theater advertise: "Tonight! The Tragedy of HAMLET, the Prince of Denmark." And, "HAMLET IN BALTIMORE." Carriages, coaches, and landaus are driving up to the theatre entrance with wealthier audience members, so that they may have to do as little walking as possible. Many people arrive on foot, mostly carrying umbrellas as the sky is covered by large black clouds, back-lit by the full moon.

The corridor leading to the dressing rooms is crowded with actors, their helpers, and maids carrying the freshly ironed costumes. Reynolds is struggling to get through the horde of his colleagues and employees who are walking on and off the stage. He carries a small bouquet of flowers in one hand and in the other hand, high above the crowds, he carries a blue flask. He stops by the door marked "Mr. and Mrs. Poe," carefully lowers the flask, makes sure that it is tightened, and slips it in his pocket. Then, without knocking, he enters. The dressing room actually consists of two smaller interconnected rooms. In one of them, Mr. Poe paces nervously, reciting the lines of his soliloquy. He does this over and over again, as some of the words seem to slip his nervous mind. He is wearing a black costume, more reminiscent of the fashion of the 1820s, but he still looks romantic, with his pale longish pale face framed by a white ruffle of his shirt.

In the larger front room, Mrs. Poe is being helped into her white dress with a pink satin ribbon just below her bosom. Letitia is doing the last moment adjustments, making sure that Mrs. Poe clearly stands out like the star of the company. There is a bouquet of flowers prepared in a vase on the table, ready for Ophelia's mad scene. It is made up of columbines, daisies, and pansies. There is a tense atmosphere in both rooms, as usual before a major premiere. The only one who is not nervous is little five-year-old Eddy, who sits on a chair in his father's half of the room and watches all the goings-on with a curious mind of a child smart for his age.

Uninvited, and unnoticed, Mr. Reynolds enters in the midst of all this madness. He is wearing narrow black pants and a carmine red frock, to remind us of the blood his character of Claudius spills when he kills his brother, Hamlet's father. The costume is of Reynold's own design, and is not exactly of the Elizabethan period, but makes Reynold's sickly white face look chilling.

Mrs. Poe sits in her low cut white brocade dress going through her lines in her head. She looks even more beautiful as her head is bent over the small book of Shakespeare's play. On her bare neck, the narrow silver chain with a cross glistens in the kerosene light. Reynolds pretends not to notice it, but he is drawn by the image. "So, the big night is upon us. How are you feeling? I am nervous myself. Ahh, here is the boy. I saw him yesterday watching the rehearsal. He seemed to know every word by heart." Suddenly he turns to Edgar. "Tell me what you want to do when you grow up? A new Thalma, David, Garrick, Kean?"

Eddy watches nervously as the theater's director approaches him. He is fascinated by Reynold's sharp teeth that show when he smiles at the boy. Eddy almost starts crying, but Reynolds suddenly makes an about face and walks to Edgar's mother. "Remind me, Mrs. Poe, to let him play a prince when we do Richard III. Here is something for you." He gives her the bouquet of flowers he brought.

"Letitia," Mrs. Poe orders, "Bring me a shawl. It is breezy here." Letitia looks at Mr. Reynolds, but then slowly shuffles out. Mrs. Poe then turns her attention back to Mr. Reynolds. "Thank you. That was very sweet of you."

"Tonight is the night. Your husband gets his wish. I hope that you shall heed mine." he whispers. He then notices that Mr. Poe looked up from his text and is looking at him and Mrs. Poe in the adjoining room directly across. "Well, I shall not keep you." Mr. Reynolds says rather loudly. I still have a beard to glue." Reynolds gets up and walks to the smaller dressing room that belongs to Mr. Poe. He points to Eddy who sits on his chair silently watching the proceedings. He addresses Mr. Poe and announces, "That boy will make it big. Mark my words." Then, he reaches inside his costume and pulls out something from the breast pocket. It is a small bottle, made out of blue iridescent glass. "Here is something to calm down your first night jitters."

Mr. Poe takes a short look and turns away. "Thank you. I shall not drink, as I promised to stay sober."

There is an ugly sneer in Reynold's face, but Mr. Poe is too preoccupied to notice it.

"Well, as you wish. But just in case, I will leave it here by the mirror."

Mr. Poe is alone by the makeup table. The shiny blue flask in front of him is tempting. The label reads, "You are the Prince Tonight." He tries to brush his mustache with a tiny comb. Finally he can no longer abstain, and takes a small drink. Someone knocks on the door. Mr. Poe suddenly realizes that Edgar has seen him drinking and he overcompensates for his guilt by yelling to the stranger behind the door. "What is it?" The hunchback stage manager looks in.

"Mr. Poe, five minutes. Mrs. Poe still has a few more minutes."

"Thank you, Wilburn."

He stands up, goes to his wife, embraces her, and kisses her. She seems a bit distant tonight—probably performance night nerves. "Break a leg, darling. This night belongs to you." Poe picks up Edgar and kisses his forehead. Then he throws his short cape over his shoulder and starts walking out, but stops himself, returns to the room, takes the flask, and puts it in his pocket. He walks backstage where he has to avoid his fellow actors, embracing each other and spitting over each other's shoulders for good luck.

The lights at the theatre auditorium are finally being dimmed by a number of stage hands, who have to walk to each light and lower or shut it down. The curtain goes up on a romantic decoration of the castle Elsinore. The backdrop hanging has a moonlit scene painted on it. As the first scene starts, some of the late-comers are being seated. Among the audience members sitting in one of the front rows is Mr. Lowell.

Little Eddy sits in the stage wings right next the prompter. He watches the scene with as much concentration of which a wise beyond his age child is capable. He repeats quietly all the lines. "Rosemary, that's for remembrance…"

His mother, as Ophelia, declaims her lines:

OPHELIA

Pray, love, remember: And

there are pansies for thoughts."

Eddy repeats after her, "Pray, love, remember…" He can see the actor who plays Laertes is pacing on the stage.

LAERTES

"A document in madness, thoughts and remembrances fitted."

OPHELIA

"There is fennel for you, and columbines.

There's rue for you.

She hands some flowers to Eddy's Hamlet Father. Then she turns away from him and turns into the audience which sits in complete silence.

OPHELIA

"And here's some for me;-

we may call herb grace o' Sundays;

By now Eddy fell asleep in his chair.

It is intermission and Mr. Poe, dressed in his Hamlet costume and makeup, comes to Eddy and whispers in his ears. "Do you like it?" Edgar nods enthusiastically. "Just two more acts and then you go home with your mother and Leticia."

Mrs. Poe as Ophelia is dead by now, but that doesn't stop her from coming back downstage and taking a deep bow when the audience applauds wildly. Several bouquets are thrown in her direction. She catches a bouquet of white roses and throws it back into the audience. Lowell lunges and catches it. He smiles at Mrs. Poe, who then returns to play the dead Ophelia again. Reynolds, sitting on the throne dressed as King Claudius, watches Mr. Poe.

He whispers to himself, while smoothing his fake beard, "Good night, sweet prince!"

Hamlet is a long play. On stage is the Churchyard scene—a painted scenery of a romantic moonlit night behind the church. Mr. Poe is on stage again, this time contemplating the skull of his faithful jester, Yorick.

HAMLET

"That skull had a tongue in it and

could sing once; how the knave jowl

it to the ground that did the murder."

Mr. Poe's face is pale and he seems to be sweating profusely. He wipes his brow with his sleeve but goes on with his monologue.

HAMLET

"This might be a pate of a politician

which this ass now overreaches:

That would circumvent God, might it not?"

Mr. Smithson, who plays Horatio, notices that something is wrong, but he stays in character.

HORATIO

"It might, my Lord."

Meanwhile, actors who are not in the scene are watching from the wings. They are queuing up to be part of Ophelia's funeral procession. There stands the Queen, Laertes, Mr. Reynolds as Claudius, and priests. Mr. Reynolds motions to Mrs. Poe to follow him. She is all painted white and pale as the dead Ophelia, but follows him to a secluded place behind some flats. Reynolds is obsequious. "You were magnificent my dear. Here is a token of my appreciation and our future collaboration." He opens a small box covered by crimson velvet and takes out a black ribbon with a large red ruby in the middle. He starts tying it around Mrs. Poe's neck despite her protestations.

"How do I deserve such a beautiful thing?" asks Mrs. Poe.
"You richly deserve it. Just bow your head and take off that chain. The time is short.

Without much thinking, Mrs. Poe removes Mr. Lowell's little cross and Reynolds ties the black velvet ribbon in the back of her long neck. When he is done, Mrs. Poe lifts her head and shakes her rich black hair. "Beautiful." says Mr. Reynolds admiringly.

Musicians are playing a funeral dirge and the funeral procession is ready to enter the stage but they are waiting for their dead Ophelia.

"This is our cue. They surely must be waiting." Both of them hurry to the stage entrance. Mrs. Poe quickly presses the little chain and a cross to her son's hand.

"Here Eddy. Hold this for your mommy. In another minute, I'll come back to get you. Pallbearers pick her up and carry on stage. They stop in front of Mr. Poe.

HAMLET

"The queen, the courtiers; who is

that they follow? And with such

maimed rites?

Lowell, forgetting that he is just part of the audience tonight, keeps moving his lips unconsciously with Hamlet's speeches. Suddenly, Ophelia is being lowered to the ground and Lowell notices that something has changed from the previous scene. He takes his opera glasses from his lap and notices that Mrs. Poe's silver cross he gave her is gone. Instead, there is a gleaming jewel that replaced his gift. Lowell gets up and starts working his way through the row of irritated audience. He can hardly hear that the play continues on stage:

HAMLET

"What, sweet Ophelia!

QUEEN

Sweets to sweets! Farewell!"

Lowell manages to get out of the auditorium and tries the backstage entrance, but the door is locked. He proceeds to run out of the theatre. It is a cold night outside. Lowell runs around the building to the actors' entrance. He bumps into a lady selling bouquets of pansies and violets. The woman falls down and the flowers from her basket are strewn in the muddy road. Apologizing, Lowell helps to pick up the flowers and place them back into the basket. "Forgive me. I didn't see you. Here is a coin for your trouble." The actor's entrance is also locked as everyone is backstage watching Mr. Poe's performance. All that Mr. Lowell can hear are the "Trumpet's sound and cannon shot off," as Shakespeare wrote.

On the stage, Reynolds sits as King Claudius on a throne surrounded by courtiers. Mr. Poe is quite good when they exchange their rapiers with Laertes. Hamlet wounds Laertes, not knowing that his sword was poisoned. As the fight goes on, Mr. Poe is performing the rehearsed movements, but he seems to have lost all his energy and is only going through the motions. He turns to Mr. Reynolds and under his breath he tries to talk to him. "I am not feeling well."

"Just go on. You can't stop now." Mr. Reynolds whispers. Standing up, he continues.

CLAUDIUS

"Part them. They are incens'd."

Mr. Poe can no longer control himself. "It seems all's going dark." he utters. The prompter tries to whisper the next sentence as loud as possible without being heard.

"Nay, come again."

Eddy is looking at the stage and at the prompter, who is panicking. He senses that something is going wrong. Suddenly the Queen falls on the ground.

OSRIC

"Look, the Queen there ho!"

HORATIO

"They bleed on both sides. How is it,

my lord?"

Pause. The audience is disconcerted. When the silence is too long, the actress playing the Queen opens her eyes to see what is happening. Then, Mr. Poe's voice can be heard as he yells at the prompter.

"Cue! My memory is gone!"

Reynolds (as Claudius) walks towards Mr. Poe and hisses, "Remember your fans..."

Among the stage hands and actors gathered in the wings watching the goings on is also Mrs. Poe. She is terrified and just clutches the ruby hanging on her neck. Edgar wants his mother to pick him up, but she is too nervous. "Not now, Eddy! Letitia, do something for God's sake.

I can't now."

Letitia picks up Eddy and holds him tight. "If you'll be quiet, Letitia will tell you a story."

"Something scary?"

Letitia takes one more look at the stage and carries Edgar away. "Yes, something scary again."

Mr. Poe gathered enough strength to lean against the wings. The actor playing the dying Laertes is leaning against a prop balcony on stage and nervously eyes Mr. Poe.

LAERTES

"Why as a woodcock to my own

prince, Osric. I am justly kill'd

With mine own treachery."

Mr. Poe answers mechanically, just trying to get through with his lines.

HAMLET

"How is..

He pauses, trying to catch his breath.

...the Queen?"

CLAUDIUS

"She swoons to see them bleed."

Reynolds keeps watching Mr. Poe holding on to the wing curtain.

QUEEN

"No, no, the drink,

Oh my dear Hamlet"

At that moment Mr. Poe remembers the flask. He looks at Reynolds and reaches to his pocket to pull out the blue flask. Reynolds watches him without emotions. The actress playing Hamlet's mother, the Queen, tries to throw Mr. Poe the next line, hoping that he will remember the rest. She is at the edge of panic. This was supposed to be the great opening night to which they were all looking forward.

QUEEN

"The drink, the drink, I am poisoned."

The Prompter is searching through his pages, lost.

HAMLET

The drink, I am poisoned."

The Prompter finally found the next line.

PROMPTER

"Oh, villainy! Ho! Let the door be locked."

Lowell is pounding on the door and finally attracts the attention of the Stage Manager, who opens the actor's entrance for him. "Mr. Lowell, I am not allowed to let you…" Mr. Lowell doesn't take no for an answer and keeps walking down the hallway to the stage. The Prompter keeps repeating that "Mr. Reynolds doesn't allow…" but by then Mr. Lowell is gone in the labyrinth that is the theatre. By now, the duel scene on stage is finally over.

HAMLET

"Treachery … Seek it out."

Laertes falls. To the surprise of those in the audience who know the play, Hamlet falls too. The actor who plays Laertes lies in a supine position and is by now very nervous.

LAERTES

"It is here, Hamlet. Hamlet thou

art slain. No medicine in the world

can do thee good. In thee there is

not half an hour of life."

Mr. Poe, short of breath, pulls out the flask out of his pocket and lifts it for everyone to see. The audience is laughing, thinking that the actor is inebriated. Laertes tries to speak louder, to overpower the giggles.

LAERTES

"Never to raise again, thy mother

poisoned. I can no more. The king,

the king's to blame.

Mr. Poe turns towards the stage hands in the wing and implores them under his breath, "Curtain, lower the curtain!"

Reynolds, still in character as Claudius, walks up to Hamlet and, with his back to the audience, he tries to prop Mr. Poe against a chair.

"Keep going you fool. Just a few more minutes. Then do what you will."

The other actors on the stage are trying to cover up the long pauses which makes the whole proceedings even more of a shambles. The Prompter is by now near hysterics. He no longer cares if the audience can hear him. "The point is envenomed too," he yells at Mr. Poe.

OSRIC

"Treason! Treason."

Only Mr. Reynolds keeps a calm head.

KING CLAUDIUS

"O yet defend me friends; I am

the one!"

Reynolds looks into the wings and sees Mrs. Poe, who in her pallor looks even more beautiful. She is clearly not well. He smiles at her. She suddenly understands and can hardly muffle a cry.

Mr. Poe collects his strength, and sitting with his back against the chair that Reynolds put him in, he manages to collect his strength and tries for the last monologues. He keeps missing his lines, but after what was just a mediocre Hamlet, his words become moving and beautiful. The audience is moved and some sobs can be heard, when the soliloquy is over.

HAMLET

"I am sad, Horatio... Wretched

Queen, adieu. You that look pale

and tremble at this chance... To

tell the story... For in that sleep

of death... What dreams may come..

Angels and ministers grace defend

"us.. To die, to sleep-- HELP SOMEONE!

I AM DYING! The fair Ophelia..."

Then there is absolute silence in the theatre. The curtain falls. There is pandemonium behind the curtain. Mrs. Poe has fainted. Everyone runs to see what's ailing Mr. Poe. A stagehand holds Mr. Poe's head in his lap. Unnoticed, Reynolds picks up Mrs. Poe. He stops by Letitia who is covering Eddy's eyes with her large hands. "Take care of the boy," he orders Letitia. "I'll take Mrs. Poe to her room." He then exits with Mrs. Poe's lifeless body in his arms.

Mr. Lowell missed this scene, as he was preoccupied by the discovery of the blue flask that Mr. Poe let fall out of his hand as he was dying. He picks it up and sniffs the contents. He yells, "Strychnine!" but no one pays attention to him. He reads the label which says, "You are the prince tonight. Reynolds." He stands up, searching through the people around him.

"REYNOLDS!"

No one pays attention, except for Letitia who answers, "He took Mrs. Poe to safety." Mr. Lowell's eyes widen.

Suddenly, a blood curdling scream is heard. It's coming from the dressing rooms. Lowell runs towards Poe's dressing room, but when no one opens it, he has to break down the door to get in. He can see that the mirror in the wall is turning.

Mrs. Poe lies in the bed unconscious. She is covered by blood. Her beautiful neck has bites marks gushing red liquid. Its color matches the ruby on her necklace.

While several other actors gather in the small dressing room, Lowell looks for a spring that could open the secret passage behind the mirror. By chance, he pulls on the little gilded carved putti on the wall and the mirror swings open. Lowell takes a candlestick and runs into the underground passage that was hidden behind the mirror. He sees Reynolds running in front of him in the dark, wet corridor. Suddenly Reynolds seems to have more energy, as if he had become younger. The grounds are wet and they are disturbing rats that lived in the dank spaces. They pass under a sewage outflow and Mr. Lowell has to try to avoid the cesspool that is flowing down the walls of the passageway. Lowell manages to escape mostly unharmed by the sewage that was pouring from the ceiling. His candle went out, but he is holding on to the candlestick as a weapon now.

Several of Mrs. Poe's fellow actors and actresses are trying to console the dying Mrs. Poe. The actress who played the Queen is wiping the blood off Mrs. Poe's face which, by now, is even paler than at other times. Mrs. Poe still finds energy to look for her son. "Where is Eddy? I want to see him before I die."

The Queen looks around at the other actors, but they are all helpless. A couple of them are crying. "Nonsense, sweetheart, you will be alright again."

Mrs. Poe smiles sadly. The actor playing Laertes runs inside. He announces, "The doctor will be here momentarily, and the police are also on the way."

Mrs. Poe can't hear any of this. "Eddy. Where is my child?"

Letitia pushes Eddy through the crowd to stand next to his mother. He is visibly terrified.

Letitia picks Eddy up. "Kiss your mother, Master Eddy."

Edgar starts crying and tries to free himself from Letitia's grip. Letitia is helpless, but the older actress portraying the Queen won't have any of it.

"You have heard, child! Kiss your mother's cheeks."

With the help of two other actors, she puts the screaming and kicking boy against his mother's face. Eddy frees himself and runs away.

Mr. Lowell meantime finds himself in the space under the stage. It's dark there except the few strips of light penetrating through the openings between the wooden planks. Suddenly, the huge wheel that is supposed to move the turntable on the stage starts slowly moving around, almost crushing Lowell in the process. He manages to jump into the corner of the room, thus avoiding the wooden behemoth. He can hear Reynolds's laughter and voice. "Get out of my way, Lowell. There is one dead Hamlet on the stage already. Do you want to be the next?"

Suddenly Lowell notices a black cat running in the direction of the open coffin at the other end of the low ceilinged room. Lowell is faster. He slams down the coffin lid, thus preventing the cat from hiding inside of it, He grabs the animal. The cat thrashes around violently, but it can't reach Lowell, who keeps it at arm's length. Lowell wants to take the cat upstairs, but as he reaches for the candlestick he left on the floor, he loses balance and his grip on the cat in the process.

In an instant, Reynolds stands next to Lowell, picks up the candlestick, and blows on it. Immediately the candles are ablaze again. Holding the candlestick in one hand, Reynolds starts climbing a rope ladder that leads to the fly space, holding on to the ropes with his remaining hand. When Lowell tries to follow him, Reynolds tries to throw the burning candles at him. Lowell dodges the fiery objects, and a candle falls on the curtain and fabric starts burning.

Lowell chases Reynolds on the bridge. The two men slide and skid down the ropes onto the stage where there are still weapons left over from the performance of Shakespeare's Hamlet. Lowell stoops down to pick up a sword, but Reynolds already has his sword prepared on ready. While the two men are dueling, their silhouettes are backlit by the large backdrops of the palace burning around them.

The doctor has finally arrived and tries to take Mrs. Poe's pulse, but he can only confirm that she is dead. "We are too late. There is no help I can give her. What a terrible death. It looks as if a wild animal bit on that lovely neck."

Letitia makes a sign of cross on herself. Several actors are crying. Eddy runs into the next room. The doctor looks around and makes his final announcement. "Mrs. Elisabeth Poe died at midnight of December, 8, 1814."

Just at that moment when the gathered actors turn to leave, the young actor who played Horatio runs in screaming, "FIRE! Save yourself!"

All the actors are trying to escape through the narrow exit door, except for Letitia who starts looking for Eddy. "Master Edgar...Eddy where are you? Eddy! The theatre is on fire. We must run!" She realizes that Eddy is hiding under the makeup table. "Come on out Eddy!" She bends down to grab him, but Eddy bites her hand. "Eddy, this is not time for games!"

Eddy starts screaming. Letitia is getting impatient. "Come. Don't you feel the smoke?"

Then, just as she bends down again to lift the kicking boy, Letitia realizes that Mrs. Poe stands behind her on the bed, all covered by blood. Mrs. Poe, like a somnambulist, raises her arms. "My boy! My boy!

At that moment Letitia lets out a blood curdling cry. "CARMELLA LEE!!!" She then runs out of the room, forgetting about the child she is leaving behind.

The flames are bursting through the roof. Actors and others are standing at a safe distance, watching the destruction. Lowell runs out of the door.

"Where is the child?

The Queen yells back, bewildered. "Their nanny had him...where is..."

At that moment they hear Letitia screaming. She runs out of the building and faints on the stairs. Lowell sees that she came alone and barks at the Queen. "Take care of her!" He runs into the theatre again. The halls are filled with smoke. He shouts, "Eddy! Eddy!" He runs into the Poe's dressing rooms. The bed where Mrs. Poe was lying is now empty. He hears crying. Under his father's dressing table is a little boy. He is covering his head with his hands in which he still holds the little silver cross. Eddy has a terrified expression in his face, even long after Mr. Lowell picks him up. "Everything will be fine now. Come let's leave fast." He finds a pitcher with water and pours it on one of the costumes hanging on the folding screen. He covers the boy's head with it and he runs out with the child in his arms, out of the room, through the fiery corridor, into the safety of the street.

The smoke is covering the once beautiful building. The gold covered sculptures on the balconies are peeling. On the empty stage lies the body of David Poe, "The Hamlet of Baltimore." A large painted backdrop of Elsinore falls down and buries him. It's dawn outside and firemen and some neighbors who formed a bucket brigade are trying to save at least the outer shell of the burned out building. Lowell is standing nearby, exhausted. The boy is holding on to him steadfastly. Letitia is sitting on the ground next to them, mumbling something to herself.

Mr. Lowell takes Eddy in his arms again. "You see, Edgar. Your parents wanted more than what they were destined to have. When you grow up, you will forgive them their greed and human pride."

The first rays of sun appear above the smoldering ruins of the theatre. On the remaining piece of the roof stand two large black cats. Mr. Lowell notices them. "Come, Letitia. Let's get the child to a warm bed." Lowell is walking across the square, taking the little boy home. Letitia goes behind them, holding in one hand the little silver cross on a chain. In her other hand, she carries the white brocade dress that Eddy's mother wore as Ophelia. This time it covered Eddy as a protection against the fire.

Two black cats are walking down a deserted square. Only the hunchback stage manager stands by the burned main entrance. He takes off the wall a poster that has miraculously survived. It says in large block letters:

TONIGHT: HAMLET IN BALTIMORE

CPSIA information can be obtained
at www.ICGtesting.com
Printed in the USA
LVHW070232010321
680231LV00003B/17